The TUTTI FRUTTI Connection

written by Alan Cameron

illustrated by Steve Romney

A Noodle Factory Children's Book Club
Presentation
1980

1

The screen door slammed as Penny came out into the backyard with two dollars in her hand. She carefully folded the bills and tucked them into the front pocket of her jeans.

"Mark!" she called up into the leafy branches of an old apple tree. "You want to go for ice cream? I got money from Mom."

"What does she want ice cream for? There's some in the freezer."

"Yeah smarty, but no tutti-frutti. And Mom wants some for dinner tonight. You better get down here if you want to go. I'm leaving right now." Penny turned and walked around the house toward the street.

"Coming! I'm coming!" A pair of tan legs appeared, hanging from a tree branch. The legs dropped quickly to the ground. The curly-headed boy hurried after his sister.

"How much money you got?" he panted when he caught up with her.

"Enough," replied Penny. "We can each get a cone after we get the tutti-frutti."

"An ice cream cone! I scream, you scream, we all scream for ice cream!" Mark rhymed happily. He danced backward down the sidewalk in front of Penny.

"You're so funny," Penny frowned at a spot six inches above Mark's head. She swished her ponytail and started walking faster. Mark almost tripped trying to get out of her way.

I wish Mark would grow up, Penny thought. He's always acting so goofy. If he were more like me, we could get along better. He's only ten. But if he doesn't start now, he'll never grow up.

Penny walked along with her chin up and her head tilted back. She looked at the world in a cool, determined way. Her look seemed to say, I know where I'm going and no mistake. For twelve years old, she told herself, I've already got a lot of my future figured out. I've got plans!

Mark paid no attention to Penny's grown-up airs. He hopped and skipped along behind her, looking down at his feet. First he tried to land on every crack. Then he switched to landing anywhere except on a crack. He was jumping completely over every other square when he crashed into Penny, who was standing on the corner looking down Elm Street.

"Ow! Watch it, Mark," she yelled at him, rubbing her shoulder.

"Hey!" Mark cried, ignoring his sister. "Look at the new ice cream shop!"

"That's just what I was doing before you so rudely interrupted me," Penny snapped. She headed down Elm Street toward the brightly painted red and white building. A big sign shaped like an ice cream cone hung over the door. Little planets orbited around the top of the ice cream. Below the cone the sign read Trip Dip.

"Hey, I want to go down to Dairy Delight and get some chocolate chip," Mark called after her.

"You can go if you want," Penny said without turning her head. "But I'm holding on to the money."

Mark frowned and kicked a pebble into the street. Then he trotted after his sister. "You know," he told her as they pulled open the store's front door, "they must have put this place up pretty quick. I'm almost sure there wasn't any store here yesterday."

"That just goes to show how much you notice," Penny told him. She thought to herself, I don't remember seeing anything new along Elm Street recently, either.

No one else was in the shop. Penny and Mark looked through the glass top of the freezer at the open buckets of ice cream. There were several color combinations they hadn't seen in ice cream before. They saw purple, green dots in dark blue, red and black checkerboard. They even saw what looked like little blue lightning bolts in vanilla.

Mark read off the names of some of the flavors. "Electro Chocolate. Mystery Matrix. Wild Blue Yonder. Chartmap Chip. These are pretty strange, Penny. Have you ever tasted Strawberry Warp?"

Penny was looking at the wall behind the counter. It seemed to tremble just a bit every few seconds, as if a wave were passing through it. "Gosh, I don't think. . ." She was interrupted by a large, smiling bald-headed man in a long striped apron. He came bustling out of the back room.

"Ah, customers, customers! That's what we like to see! How may I serve you, young gentleman and lady?"

"Well, we were looking for tutti-frutti, actually. A packed quart," Penny told him.

"Oh? I hope you won't think I'm shirking my duty. But I've never heard of any ice cream called—what did you say?—tutti-frutti."

"Never heard of tutti-frutti?" Mark asked in surprise. "That's weird."

"We'll just have to get it somewhere else," Penny told him. She turned back to the shopkeeper. "I'd like to try one of your new flavors." She took out her money and carefully separated the two dollar bills. "Could I have a single scoop of Meteoric Mint, please."

The bald shopkeeper beamed down at her. He wiped his hands on his apron and reached for an empty cone. "Surely, surely. What's yours, Curly?" He favored Mark with the same big smile.

"How come you talk so funny?" Mark asked.

"Don't be rude, Mark," Penny told him sternly. "Just tell him what you want."

"Oh, that's all right, miss," the shopkeeper replied. "I don't mind a bit. I've always talked this way and I just can't quit."

"Um." Mark looked up at the shopkeeper doubtfully. "Well, I usually have chocolate chip, or sometimes hot fudge. But you haven't got either, as far as I can judge."

6

"Ah, very good, very good! You speak as one should." The bald shopkeeper looked surprised and pleased. He put down his scoop. He backed away from the counter, feeling along the wall behind him with his hand. "We've got lots to choose from, young man, lots to pick. But I haven't got all day, so let's make it quick."

Mark was enjoying this conversation by now. "It's been a while since I had lunch, so I guess I'll try Galactic Crunch."

"Right," answered the bald shopkeeper. He was smiling as widely as ever. He pressed a button on the wall behind him. "Hold tight," he said. That was the last thing Penny and Mark heard. Then a bright pink cloud swirled around them. And the ice cream shop started rattling and shaking.

Penny and Mark gasped and coughed. They tried to wave the pink cloud away. When it finally cleared, the bald shopkeeper leaned over the counter and handed them each an ice cream cone. Penny noticed that hers didn't look like any cone she'd ever seen before.

She gave the shopkeeper a dollar. "You ought to do something about your air conditioning," she told him. "That pink cloudy stuff is awful."

But she saw he wasn't paying any attention to her. He was peering intently at the dollar bill she had given him. It's almost as if he's never seen one before, she thought. The shopkeeper turned the bill over and gave a start. "Aaah!" he gasped, staring at it in fright.

7

"What's the matter?" Penny asked.

The shopkeeper dropped the dollar as if it were red hot. He rushed through the door to the back room of the store. Penny and Mark heard a crash. It sounded like a lot of things falling on the floor. Then they heard a door slam. The shopkeeper had run out on them!

"What's he so scared of?" Penny wondered.

"Probably afraid we'd ask for our money back," Mark told her. "This ice cream tastes weird. Yuck!"

Penny still hadn't tried hers. She walked around behind the counter and poked her head into the back room. It was dark and quiet. Then she saw the dollar lying on the floor where the shopkeeper had been standing. No sense in letting it go to waste, she thought. She stooped to pick it up.

"Oh my gosh! Look at that!" Mark exclaimed. "Something's happened!" Penny tucked the dollar carefully back in her pocket and walked back around the counter. Mark was staring out the front window. His eyes were wide. Elm Street had disappeared!

Everything had disappeared. There were no cars, no trucks, no buses, no buildings. And no people. There was nothing. Penny gulped hard.

Then she saw that there was something. It was a big, blank gray wall barely two feet away. It was so smooth and gray and close to the window that it looked like a big empty space. It crowded right up to the front of the store, as if it were about to fall in on it. The wall must be blocking out Elm Street, Penny thought. But how did it pop up so fast? And how, she suddenly remembered with a start, had the ice cream shop been built so quickly?

By pressing her face to the glass, Penny could see that the wall stretched far out of sight above them. At the base of the wall, in the narrow space between it and the store, two small conveyor belts ran smoothly along. One went to the left and one went to the right.

"What happened?" Penny wondered aloud after several moments of wide-eyed silence.

"That's a good question," replied Mark. He frowned at the ice cream cone in his hand. "Maybe it's some kind of special contest."

"Oh, cut it out Mark! Can't you see this is serious? We'd better call home right away." Penny looked around the shop for a pay phone. She didn't see one. She dashed behind the counter. But there was no phone there either.

"Let's just stay calm for a minute now, Mark," Penny said. She slowly returned to the front of the store. "The best thing is just to stay put and stay calm—Mark?" But Mark had already stepped outside.

Penny rushed to the front door and opened it a crack. "Mark!" she hissed. Her brother stood in the narrow alley peering up and down the rolling conveyor belts. "Get back in here this instant!"

"There's nothing in there, Sis," he complained. "Nothing but a lot of bad-tasting ice cream.

9

C'mon, let's check this out. Maybe these things go around the wall, back to Elm Street." With that, he hopped onto one of the conveyor belts and started moving away.

"Mark!" Penny called one last time. But he just kept rolling. Penny shrugged, then slipped out the door. She stepped up onto the moving belt. I guess we're not going to stay put, she thought. But we'd better stay together. And what about staying calm, she reminded herself. She tried to relax, but couldn't. Her stomach felt tight, and her throat too. She just hoped they could get back to Elm Street without any problem.

The conveyor belt carried them past the ice cream shop. Where the shop ended, another gray wall began. Mark and Penny were now rolling along between two smooth, blank walls that rose high above them. It felt like being down in a deep mine.

Penny took a few steps. She found she could walk on the rolling belt if she went slowly and kept her balance. "I sure hope this gets us to Elm Street," she told Mark as she caught up with him. "We really should have stayed back there. If we get in trouble it'll be all your fault."

"My fault?" cried Mark. "You were the one who wanted to go into that stupid place. The Trip Dip! Huh! It's not even. . ."

Mark was cut short when the two walls came to an end. The conveyor belt rolled them out into the open. They both gasped in astonishment. Before them stretched a vast network of conveyor belts rolling along in every direction. On the belts, people singly and in groups were carried to and fro. Everyone wore bright, shiny clothes. The whole scene was one of dazzling, shifting, changing colors.

Off in the distance were tall buildings. There were more skyscrapers than Penny had ever seen. She looked back at the walls they had come through. They weren't walls at all, but big windowless buildings. Giant blocks of concrete surrounded the ice cream shop.

This sure isn't Elm Street, Penny realized. We must be a million miles from there! Where on earth are we? We'd better find out how to get back quick, or we're in real trouble!

Penny and Mark edged backwards. They didn't want to be drawn into the strange crowd before them. But there was no going back. The belt carried them on.

Soon it merged with a larger, wider belt. Penny and Mark could stand side by side, with room to spare. All around them other belts carried people in shiny suits at different speeds and in different directions. Penny and Mark stared at them. The people stared back.

They seemed to be fascinated most of all by Mark's and Penny's heads. Or by their hair. Mark's hair was thick and curly. Penny's was tied back in a ponytail. The people in the shiny suits were all completely bald.

Penny stared in disbelief at several bald-headed women who passed by. Then she started

11

to notice other things about the people riding the belts. Their shiny, colored suits were all in one piece. And in addition to being bald, the people wearing the suits were also barefoot.

The people were beginning to notice Penny's and Mark's clothes too. They pointed at Mark's red soccer shorts and his blue tennis shoes. They stared at Penny's sandals, her blue jeans and her yellow shirt.

"It's like one of those dreams," whispered Mark. "You're sitting at your desk in school. Suddenly you realize you forgot to get dressed that morning. Only. . ." he drifted off, ". . .not quite. Penny, I'm really scared!" he suddenly blurted out.

"If only we could wake up home in bed," said Penny. "I've been pinching myself ever since that man disappeared. But it doesn't seem to do any good."

Their talk was cut off by shouts off to the right. They saw someone waving at them, hopping from belt to belt. The figure elbowed through groups of people. Penny could tell that it was a woman, bald head and all. She was wearing a turquoise-colored suit. First she moved in the same direction as Mark and Penny. Then she jumped to a closer track moving away from them. Next she hopped onto another belt moving along with them.

Mark turned to run off down the belt. But Penny laid a hand on his shoulder. "Wait," she said.

The tall woman in turquoise finally landed

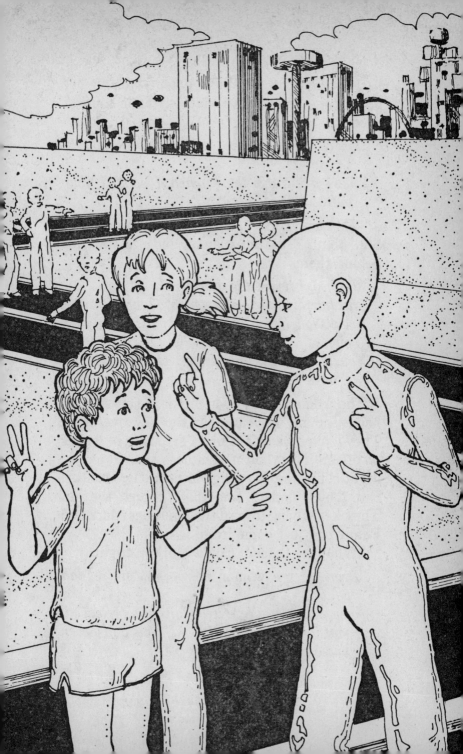

beside them on the belt. After catching her breath she said, in a funny rhythmic kind of speech:

> *"You've come from the experimental Timeworks,*
> *I suppose.*
> *I was going out there when I spotted your*
> *outrageous clothes."*

"We came from back there," Penny replied. She pointed to the blank buildings now far behind them.

> *"Just so. I heard the alarm,*
> *And hurried out to see you came to no harm.*
> *Even though you've travelled so far on your*
> *own,*
> *You won't get much further, chased by those*
> *drones."*

The woman nodded at the dark ships which had suddenly appeared in the sky overhead. They looked like giant black sausages or loaves of bread. They had no features that Penny or Mark could see. No wings or propellers or legs. But they hummed smoothly through the air. They were flying toward the buildings Mark and Penny had just come from.

"What are those?" asked Mark in fright.

> *"Drones,"* the woman answered, *"full of lab*
> *police,*
> *Answering the alarm the Timeworks released.*
> *If you will, please forgive me, you don't even*
> *know my name.*

14

I'm Dr. Kay Kayla, Hearer of History. That's why I came," she added, as if it would explain everything.

"Dr. Kayla," Penny asked slowly, with a puzzled frown, "what alarm are you talking about?"

"The one that went off in the ice cream shop,
When your experimenter decided he had to stop."

"Dr. Kayla," Penny asked again, even more slowly, "what experiment were we in?"

"It's a top secret project, but since you've asked,
You're the product of a probe far into the past.
You might be surprised to learn today's date.
We're now in the year 2468!"

2

"What?" cried Penny and Mark in shock.

"*Yes,*" Dr. Kayla told them. *"I'm afraid it's
true.
And you're in for some more surprises, you
two."*

"What are we doing here? Why are we here?"
Mark muttered. He stared at the strange scene
around him.

"But—but why? Why us? Why bring us into the
future?"

Penny felt panic race through her. "What do
they want?"

Dr. Kayla urged,

*"Try not to think of the worst, just the best,
You two are here as the results of a test.
The Timeworks machine had never been tried.
But now it has—and you have arrived!"*

"All I want to do is go back," Penny shook her
head as she spoke. "Go back home to my mom
and dad. Will they send us back right away?"

Dr. Kayla answered sadly:

*"That's something I know nothing about, my
child.*

The scientists running this are all a bit wild.
And big on secrecy—they don't explain at all.
To find out any more, we must pay them a
call."

The belt carried the three of them into the city.
The bald-headed people moving around them
still stared. Black drone ships hummed by overhead. Huge screens on the walls of some of the
buildings showed giant bald heads. The heads
were talking and smiling down on the rolling
crowds. Following Dr. Kayla, Penny and Mark
stepped off the belt in front of a shining bronze
building. As they walked toward it, they could see
that its walls were bronze-tinted mirrors reflecting
everything around them. Over the large front
doors silver letters spelled out Chamber of the
Great, and below that Directors of Development,
Controllers of Fate.

Dr. Kayla turned to Mark and Penny as they
entered the building.

"A word of caution. I know something about
your time.
I've studied it. For instance, your speech
doesn't rhyme.
But here you must always talk in a poetic way,
Or people will be insulted, no matter what you
say."

Penny just stared at her. Mark whispered, "I
knew it sounded weird." They walked down a
long hall with shining metal walls. They had
almost reached the large golden doors at the end

when Dr. Kayla stopped.

"Oh, one more thing I meant to ask.
What made that experimenter leave you so
fast?"

"I don't know, Dr. Kayla," Penny replied. "I just tried to pay him for the ice cream."

"Pay?" Dr. Kayla sounded surprised.

"Oh, of course. I nearly forgot,
Back in your day you still sold and bought."

"Of course we did," said Mark. "How else do you get something?"

"Here in our time, in our bright modern city,
You'll find many things changed. Some, a pity.
But progress and knowledge, I must confess
Have altered most of the rest for the best.
For instance, money.
We don't use it, sonny." She waggled a finger at Mark.

"Outmoded. Outdated. Old-fashioned. Obsolete.
Why, it's nearly as useless as those things on
your feet!"

Dr. Kayla stopped to catch her breath.

"Oh, I'm sorry, no offense.
But they just don't make sense."

She looked at Penny.

"One more thing before we go in, honey.
Will you let me have a look at your money?"

Penny dutifully pulled out her two dollars and handed one to Dr. Kayla.

"Paper money! Why, that's very rare!" She turned the bill over and looked startled. *"Oh, you'd better watch out! Take care!"*

"What do you mean, Dr. Kayla?" asked Penny.

Dr. Kayla handed the dollar back to her, then frowned for a moment.

"I don't have time to explain, not until this is done.
But that piece of money—don't show it to anyone!"

And with that Dr. Kayla led them through the golden doors.

Inside, groups of men and women with short black capes draped over their shiny, colored suits talked with one another. They stood around gleaming silver tables that seemed to hover in the air without legs. The tables were placed on different levels rising above the floor where Mark and Penny now stood. The levels went all the way up to the ceiling of the large room. Caped figures stood on every level. Penny felt like she was in the middle of a circus arena.

Dr. Kayla took one of the short black capes from a hook by the door and draped it over her shoulders. Then she announced to the chamber,

"Learned scientists all, it is my pleasure to present
These two young travelers from the Timeworks experiment."

Everyone looked up, then took places behind

the shimmering, floating tables. Their bald heads loomed high over Penny and Mark. A tall man in a bright purple suit stood behind a silver table directly above them. He rapped a gavel for attention. He frowned.

"I thought we sent the drones out to catch them.
Does one of our own doctors have to go fetch them?"

Besides his black cape, he also wore a strange metal hat. It was in the shape of a pyramid. The hat was made of thin silver rods. Through the rods Penny could see his bald pink scalp.

Dr. Kayla answered him:

"Doctor of Density Mac Maxta, if you please,
I met them by accident, and brought them here for you to see."

Mac Maxta frowned at her again, then said,

"Oh, really? I know we'd all feel more at ease
If you stopped interfering with the lab police.
But let's get on with business, we've questions to ask,
This is important work, our time travel task!"

"I have a question first, Your Density," Penny said. She stepped out in front of him. "When do we go back? I mean, to our own time. It better be soon or else we'll be late for dinner. Our parents will start worrying."

The council members sat in stunned silence. Then they turned to one another in anger. They

asked why this girl couldn't speak properly. Mac
Maxta pounded his gavel for order.

> *"Young lady, you're in the Chamber of the*
> *Great. Don't forget it.*
> *Show some respect or I promise you'll regret*
> *it."*

Mark stepped up beside his sister to help.

> *"We want to know*
> *How soon we can go.*
> *I can't tell you how much this visit has meant to*
> *me,*
> *But I'd really rather be back in the twentieth*
> *century!"*

This caused an immediate uproar. Council
members jumped to their feet. They were shouting
at Mac Maxta, at Mark and Penny, and at each
other. Cries of *"The boy is ungrateful! Despicable!*
Hateful!" and *"Our time is best! Forget the rest!"*
rang through the chamber. Penny noticed that a
few of the scientists had pyramids on their heads
like Mac Maxta's. They were the ones doing most
of the shouting.

Mac Maxta pounded his gavel furiously. When
order had been restored he growled down at
Mark and Penny:

> *"Do I understand you to say*
> *That you don't wish to stay?*
> *Our life here is almost too good to be true.*
> *Don't you think it would be just perfect for*
> *you?"*

"No!" answered Penny. "We want to go home!"

"No longer to roam," Mark added quickly.

"Impossible! This we will not allow!
May I remind you that we are in charge now!"
Mac Maxta thundered.

Applause and cries of *"Hear! Hear!"* came from around the chamber. Mac Maxta continued speaking.

"Now, to proceed with our plan.
It is this: young woman, young man,
You were brought here for a purpose.
Yes! Did you think this was all a big circus?
We will ask you some questions about your
*   ancient age,*
And if we decide you don't belong in a cage,
You'll be placed in a tightly controlled model
*   environment*
Under our observation from now till retirement."

"Did you get that?" Mark whispered to his sister. "They're gonna stick us in a zoo here for the rest of our lives."

"No!" Penny stamped her foot. "That's not fair!"

"Or square," Mark hurriedly put in.

Mac Maxta waved aside their complaints.

"No matter. This important project of ours must
*   at all costs succeed.*
Now, Witness of Wisdom Bar Barta, you may
*   proceed!"*

A short, fat man stood up on the very highest level of the chamber. Bar Barta wore a rumpled

24

yellow suit and a pyramid hat.

"Thank you, Doctor of Density Mac Maxta.
For my first question I would like to. . ."

"No!" cried Penny again. "Not fair or square!
You still haven't answered *my* question!"

"Or even made a suggestion," seconded Mark.

Bar Barta's face turned red. He started yelling
and pounding his fists on his shining desk. Other
scientists took up the cry. Bar Barta got so
excited that his pyramid hat toppled off his head.

Meanwhile Mac Maxta was busy restoring
order. When the chamber had quieted, Kay
Kayla stepped forward and spoke.

"Before we proceed further along this road,
I believe we should consult the Scientific Code.
Under Experimental Subjects, Subsection 8:
'After all experiments, subjects must be returned
*   to their original state.'"*

This was too much for Bar Barta, who had now
replaced his pyramid atop his head.

"Rubbish! Rubbish! I must protest!
This faulty argument can be soon laid to rest.
These two children Dr. Kayla fears so,
Really lived five hundred years ago.
Our Scientific Code protects those strong and
*   feeble.*
But it says nothing at all about rights of dead
*   people!"*

This brought more commotion around the
chamber, as members turned to debate the point

with one another. Mark muttered angrily, "I don't care what they say, I'm still alive!"

Mac Maxta once more restored order. And Dr. Kayla again stepped forward.

"In the hopes of clearing up this unlikely mess, I ask the Chamber to grant a short recess."

Mac Maxta glowered down at her. He was clearly tired of having to pound his gavel for order everytime someone made a speech. *"Very well,"* he grunted. *"Take a spell."* He smacked the gavel smartly and rose to leave the Chamber.

Kay Kayla grabbed Mark and Penny and pulled them with her toward a door in the back of the chamber. Once they were through it, she quickly locked it behind them. She led them across the small room they had entered to a door in the opposite wall.

"You must run, run and hide.
Go to my sister's, and stay inside."

"Why?" asked Penny and Mark together.

"I just found out something about the Timeworks machine.
It only works in this direction, if you know what I mean.
They brought you here all right, that was a snap.
But they haven't the faintest idea how to send you back!"

"Oh no!" cried Penny. "They can't do this to us! We've got to get back! What will our parents do?"

"We're stuck!" Mark whispered. "We'll never see them again! Not Mom or Dad or any of our friends. I'll never grow up to be a quarterback!"

"Dr. Kayla, it can't be true! You've got to make them send us back!" Penny's eyes were brimming with tears. Dr. Kayla tried to calm the two terrified children.

"I don't know how, but there must be a way.
I'll go to my own lab, start work right away.
But meanwhile you must hide, they're already mad.
And they plan to lock you up, which is twice as bad."

She hurriedly told them how to follow the rolling belts to her sister's house.

"Remember my friends, to get there: first blue border and then green.
Finally yellow to the school, then orange to one nineteen.
Now go quickly on your way.
I'll see you there in ten days." She rushed them out the door.

Mark and Penny made it safely down the dark corridor where another door opened to the outside. They looked back at Dr. Kayla, not wanting to leave her. But she waved them on. Then she disappeared back into the little room. They were on their own!

Penny and Mark opened the door and ran across an open plaza. Above them loomed a huge screen set into the wall of a skyscraper. On the

27

screen, a giant bald head nodded and smiled down on them.

"*. . .that concludes our science news and the weather.*

May you all have a pleasant evening together," the head said. Then the screen went blank. They came to a belt running out of the plaza. It had a blue border on it, just as Dr. Kayla had told them.

"What about Mom and Dad?" asked Mark as they hopped onto the blue belt. "Will they be able to find us? Do you think they've started looking for us yet?"

"I don't know." Penny tried not to sound too worried. "I doubt it. How could they find us if we're five hundred years away? We've got to look out for ourselves. Let's just concentrate on what we have to do now, Mark. This must be where we make the first switch."

Together they got off the blue belt, moved across a shiny platform, and stepped onto one bordered in green. The green belt swung away from the skyscrapers and headed out of the city. Very few people were riding now. Most of them seemed intent on getting wherever they were going. They paid little attention to Penny and Mark. The two rode a long way in silence, until Penny suddenly exclaimed:

"The dollar bill! She never explained to me about the dollar bill!"

"What about it?" Mark asked.

"Well, why it spooked that guy in the ice cream

shop, to start with. And then why did she tell us not to show it to anyone?" Penny pulled out one of the bills and examined it. She looked at the back, with the pyramid on the left and the eagle on the right. "Hey! Remember those funny hats some of them were wearing? They were shaped like pyramids!"

"Yeah!" Mark sounded doubtful. "But why would anyone be scared of a pyramid?"

"Look, the pyramid on the dollar has an eye on top of it. Weird, huh? And it has these funny words written around it."

"Do they rhyme?"

"I don't think so. *Annuit Coeptis Novus Ordo Seclorum.* Nope."

"You better put it away, Penny. She told us not to show it to anyone."

"But don't you see? This could be very important. The ancient pyramids, you know, the ones in Egypt. They're full of mystery. All kinds of stuff about secret knowledge."

Mark frowned and turned away to look at the city. There were hardly any people around. The buildings were getting smaller and the spaces between them larger.

"That looks like our next transfer up there," said Penny. She stuffed the bills back in her pocket. "Dr. Kayla said to take the yellow belt out as far as the school." They stepped off the green belt and onto a smaller yellow one.

"How are we going to recognize the school?" Mark asked. "Everything looks different here."

"We could ask someone," Penny replied. But no one else was riding the yellow belt. And they didn't see anyone walking around. All the people had vanished.

The belt carried them further from the city. The buildings on either side all looked the same: two stories high, with windows only at the top, right under the roof. Between the buildings stretched large green lawns, too brightly colored to be grass. Not a single tree or bush grew anywhere.

"There, that must be the school," Penny cried.

"How can you tell?"

"Well, look. It has a big building in the middle, and then rows of smaller buildings around it. And there's a playground, see?"

"Doesn't look like a playground to me—I don't see any swings. I think we should ride farther." But Penny had already hopped off the yellow belt. Mark followed unwillingly.

They found themselves in a large paved area surrounded by silent buildings. On one side stood a giant cube, twice Penny's height. It was made out of a lot of smaller cubes, all red, white and blue. On the other side stood a row of thin poles set in the ground, each one higher than the one before. Penny saw a seven-pointed star inside a huge circle painted on the pavement.

I know this is a playground, she thought. It has to be! I only wish there was someone around to ask for directions. Where can they all have disappeared to?

They walked on through the buildings. They came to the mouth of a long, open valley covered with bright carpeting. Houses were scattered up the valley.

Mark prodded the green surface with his toe. It was spongy and soft, but he could still walk on it. A dazzling orange stripe, about a foot wide, was painted on top of it. The orange stripe snaked up the valley between the houses. "This must be the way," said Penny. "Look for number 119."

They followed the orange stripe up the middle of the valley. On either side, the houses stood silent as stone. They had windows only at the very tops of the walls, and no doors at all. Between them stretched nothing but deserted green sponge.

"This is spooky," Mark said. "Are you sure we're in the right place?"

"We followed Dr. Kayla's directions. Her sister's house must be up here somewhere."

"But it looks like nobody lives here," Mark objected. "I mean, there's not even a dog or a cat wandering around. No bikes, no footballs lying anywhere." He suddenly stopped and looked at Penny in panic. "What if there aren't any kids in this world? Maybe they got rid of them all! Have you seen any yet?"

Penny shook her head grimly. "But there's got to be some," she said. "You saw the school back there."

"Maybe it wasn't a school for kids! That didn't look like any playground I've ever seen."

"Look, just stop worrying about everything! Think about what we have to do now—find Dr. Kayla's sister." They kept walking. After half an hour, Penny finally stopped in front of one of the silent houses. "There's no numbers, but I've been counting. This is one hundred and nineteen."

"How do we get in?" asked Mark, noting the lack of doors.

"Let's go around back."

Behind the house the surface sloped away again, still covered by the soft green carpeting. At the bottom of the hill was some kind of drainage ditch. On the other side the ground rose again. Penny guessed there were more houses on the other side of the hill.

Set into the back wall of the house were glass doors. Penny and Mark walked toward them slowly. They got just close enough to see figures behind the glass and stopped. At least somebody lived here.

The people inside were all seated on the floor, facing away from the door. They seemed to be looking at, or listening to, a blank wall opposite. But one small, bald-headed figure sat next to the glass. He was looking out with a bored expression on his face. The small face came alive with interest when it spotted Penny and Mark. The figure stood up, yanked open the glass door, and dashed out to meet them. Soft music floated from the house. Cries of protest came from those inside.

*"Not during the music hour, Ron Ronda. Oh no!
See how impossible he is? I told you so!"*

The brown-suited figure ran up to Penny and
Mark and began jabbering at them. From the
sound of the voice Penny guessed he must be a
boy. But it was hard to tell. He talked fast,
making many rhymes. Then he laughed and
touched their hair and clothes. The way he talked
sounded like nonsense to Penny. She did manage
to grasp that the boy's name was Ron Ronda.

*"Dr. Kay Kayla sent us here
To hide until the coast is clear,"* she stammered.
Ron Ronda's eyes widened at the mention of
the doctor's name. He led them into the house.

Inside, the people were reluctantly getting to
their feet. They were complaining to each other
and scolding Ron Ronda. The soothing music
was still playing, but no one paid it any attention.

The complaints soon changed to interest as
they all gathered around Penny and Mark. There
were half a dozen adults in the group. A few
children tried to crowd in to get a glimpse of the
strange visitors.

Penny tried to explain who they were. But she
soon gave up and let Mark do the talking. He was
much better at making up rhymes than she was.
And she certainly didn't want this family to get
mad at her like the scientists had.

Mark got the story across, starting with their
meeting Dr. Kayla. He left out any mention of the

twentieth century. He just said they came from another world. The group took one look at their strange clothes and hair and accepted this explanation.

One woman introduced herself as Sar Sarah, Dr. Kayla's sister. Ron Ronda was her son. Ron Ronda was very proud of having discovered Mark and Penny. He stood among the grownups, listening to everything that was said.

Sar Sarah quickly realized the danger that Mark and Penny were in. The first thing, she told them, was to get rid of their peculiar clothes and long hair. Otherwise anyone could tell they were outsiders. Garments belonging to the other children were quickly produced.

"This one's mine.

It'll fit you fine," Ron Ronda told Penny as he handed her dark blue pajamas.

"Is this a girl's suit?" Mark asked suspiciously. He held up a pink piece of clothing. *"I mean, I can't go around looking like a fruit!"*

"Oh, Mark, it doesn't make any difference. They're all the same. Just go get changed," Penny told him.

Penny slipped into the blue suit. It felt soft and comfortable. But it didn't have any pockets anywhere. She took the two dollars out of her jeans and rolled them up tightly in her hand.

Penny returned to the main room where the group was still gathered. Mark came in, dressed in pink. He whispered to Penny, "Were you in a place that looked like a bathroom? I was. At least I think so. I couldn't tell for sure."

Sar Sarah produced a large pair of scissors.

"Oh no, not my ponytail! Don't cut my hair!
"I've been growing it for a whole year. It's not
fair!" Penny cried. Then she realized what a short time that was, compared to how far from home they were. A year seemed like no time at all.

"I don't want my hair cut either.
Girl's clothes and a shaved head. I want neither!"
Mark said stubbornly.

"How about a swimming cap?
Do you have anything like that on tap?" Penny asked brightly.

They didn't know what swimming caps were, but Penny was able to explain what she wanted. Sar Sarah produced a roll of light, colored plastic. Following Penny's instructions, she cut out two pieces that could be stretched over Mark's and Penny's heads. She also cut straps to tie them on.

Penny rolled her two dollars tightly around her ponytail and snapped the elastic band over them. Then she piled all her hair on top of her head, pulled the plastic cap over it, and tied the strap under her chin. The ponytail made her new bald head kind of lumpy, but it should look all right from a distance.

The soft music filling the room suddenly stopped. The blank wall which everyone had been facing sprang to life. It became a huge color screen like the ones they had seen earlier in the city. Mac Maxta's large bald head, without the silver pyramid hat this time, filled the entire wall.

"Two dangerous prisoners have escaped. Beware!
They must be captured at once, and returned to
*   our care."*

Mac Maxta went on to describe Mark and Penny, their strange clothes and hair. He warned everyone to help in tracking them down, concluding:

"The two were last seen near Val Valley School.
Anyone hiding them is surely a fool!
Turn them in now, don't get left in the lurch.
Police are conducting a house-to-house search."

Ron Ronda was the first to move after the screen went blank. He grabbed Mark and Penny and pulled them to the glass door.

"Hurry! There's still a few hours of sunlight.
We'll get away yet—we'll give them a fight!" he said as he slid the door open. Sar Sarah was upset.

"Oh no, Ron Ronda, you must cease!
Don't get mixed up with the lab police!"

But her son was already out the door. He pushed Penny and Mark ahead of him. As they ran down the hill away from the house, they heard the steady hum of the drones in the distance.

3

Ron Ronda was first to reach the ditch at the bottom of the hill. He dropped in and turned back to look as Penny and Mark jumped in behind him. The ditch was paved, and just big enough for them to crouch down in. They all peered up over the edge, scanning the sky. Penny tugged her plastic cap tighter around her head. She hoped that from a distance, or from the air, she looked like just another bald-headed kid in a colored suit.

Ron Ronda pointed silently. Two black drone ships had appeared in the air over the valley. They flew ahead a short distance, stopping directly over one of the houses. The two drones hovered in the air together, as if talking to one another.

"How do they stay up in the air like that? They don't look like they could fly anymore than a cat," Mark whispered.

"A jet cushion float keeps them hovering up there.

They're riding on a layer of highly compressed air," Ron Ronda answered.

One drone dropped to the ground. A door in its

side opened and a dozen armed, black-suited figures stepped out. They fanned out and entered the houses in the area without knocking. The drone rose back in the air, joined its companion, and flew up the valley closer to Ron Ronda's house.

"When they've finished the houses, they'll search down here.
We'd better get going, get our escape into gear," Ron Ronda told Mark and Penny. He led them along the ditch in a crouching run.

"Where are we going? And why are you taking us?
We're perfect strangers to you. Are we worth all this fuss?" Penny asked.

Ron Ronda grinned back at her.
"Any excuse to get up and go!
My aunt sent you, that's all I need to know.
Besides, this is fun!
C'mon, we'll take the Rumble Run!"

He led them down the ditch to the mouth of a large concrete pipe. Just inside the pipe they could see a small, rickety-looking conveyor belt, patched in many places. Ron Ronda shoved first Mark, then Penny inside the pipe.

"What is this?" Penny asked Mark in a frantic whisper.

"I don't know. Water pipe, I guess," he answered her.

"That's right. And after every big rain

We must repair the belt—what a pain!
But worth it. We built it ourselves, my friends
    and I.
With spare parts we found, and some we took on
    the sly," Ron Ronda told them proudly.

He reached underneath the belt and pulled out
a small, strangely shaped wrench. He told Mark
and Penny to lie down on the belt, heading into
the pipe. Ron Ronda climbed on last and did
something with his wrench to one of the wheels
underneath the belt. The belt started moving
right away. As it carried them into the pipe it
picked up speed.

Soon they were rocketing along through the
darkness. Penny was terrified. What if they
should roll off the belt and crash into the walls of
the tunnel at top speed? What if there was
something in the tunnel blocking the way?

Penny couldn't see a thing. It was pitch black
all around. She could only hear the rapid clicking
of the belt wheels as they passed over them. She
hoped that Mark's bare feet were still inches
ahead. But she didn't dare reach out and touch
them. She might lose her balance on the thin,
swaying belt. She hoped that Ron Ronda was still
riding behind her. Without him they would be
really lost.

I still can't believe he's taking such a chance for
two people he just met, Penny thought. I guess he
really likes Dr. Kayla. She sent instructions for
the family to keep us safe. But he's really taking it
seriously!

I guess he probably just likes to run around playing cops and robbers. It's funny to think of him as just another kid when he looks so weird. And he and his friends built this underground belt from scrap—that's really something!

They went rolling rapidly on through the darkness. After a few minutes Penny saw light ahead. The thin beam broadened into a large circle. She knew they were coming to the end of the tunnel. Penny lifted her head just a little. She could see Mark lying flat on the belt in front of her. They approached the mouth of the tunnel at a fast clip. Mark reached it and in a split second popped out into the light and dropped from sight. Penny rolled to the right as she shot off the end of the belt. She didn't want to land on top of Mark when, and if, they hit the ground.

Her landing was much sooner and much softer than she expected. After only a moment in the air, she landed with a bounce on a big pile of green sponge. They were in the bottom of another ditch. Ron Ronda came out right behind her. He rolled to land on the other side of Mark.

Shaken but not hurt, Penny and Mark stood up. Ron Ronda had already scrambled back to the end of the pipe. Using his little wrench, he reached underneath the belt and shut it off.

"Pretty good ride?"
And a good way to hide," he grinned at the two of them.

Penny still thought this bald-headed boy,

41

about her size and probably her age, looked awfully funny in his brown pajama suit and bare feet. But she definitely liked him. And she realized that she desperately needed him. The scientists were all set to lock them up in a zoo. The lab police were searching everywhere for them. No one, not even Dr. Kayla, had the faintest idea of how to get them back home.

"Where are we?" asked Mark, brushing off his pink suit.

"Just behind Val Valley school.
My friends and I would rather ride than walk, as
a rule.
Climb up here, but keep your heads down.
We'll see how well they've covered this part of
town," Ron Ronda told them.

They crawled up the short rise just to the left of the ditch. Cautiously they poked their heads over the top, and looked down on the school playground they had walked through just an hour ago.

The place was swarming with drones. None of them were in the air, but a couple looked ready to take off. Lab police in black uniforms stood in groups talking. Some of them had white helmets on. All carried black sticks that looked dangerous. Penny noticed that they were all barefoot.

"This must be headquarters for the search parties in the area," whispered Mark. "We better get outta here quick."

"I hoped we could catch the belt here at the

playground.
But there's still a chance. We'll get it further down," Ron Ronda said.

They scrambled down the hill away from the school and across the ditch. Ron Ronda took them at a run across backyards and between houses.

Penny hoped that she and Mark would look like a couple of regular kids to anyone who happened to see them. Mark, running ahead of her, looked strange in his pink suit and his fake bald head.

Ron Ronda took a sharp turn between two houses. This brought them out to the yellow belt again. No one was in sight.

"Get on and lie down.
We're skipping town," Ron Ronda told them.

"But this is the kind that you ride standing up. I mean, why should we duck?" Mark protested.

Just do as I say
And we'll be on our way," Ron Ronda commanded. Penny and Mark stepped on the moving belt and lay flat. Ron Ronda stuck his wrench in one of the wheels under the belt. Then he hopped on not too far behind them. As soon as he lay down, the belt began to pick up speed.

Soon they were moving along even faster than they had been back in the tunnel. The rush of air brought tears to Penny's eyes. She turned her head and tucked her chin down to get her face out of the wind. Over her shoulder she could see Ron

44

Ronda. He was flat on his stomach, inching along the belt to catch up to her.

After a while the belt began to slow down again. When it had fallen back to its normal speed, Ron Ronda jumped up and trotted down the belt ahead of Penny and Mark. He jumped off next to another belt moving off in a different direction. Here they repeated the process. Penny and Mark got on and lay down. As they were moving away, Ron Ronda stuck his wrench into the wheels underneath the belt. Then he hopped on too. The belt took them at top speed to another part of the city where they transferred again.

Ron Ronda explained that he could only make the belts speed up for a short period of time.

"Annoying is something I don't want to be.
But where are we going, we fugitive three?"
Penny asked.

"To a place I've never been, to a place no one goes.
We should be safe there, but then—who knows?"
Ron Ronda answered with a shrug.

"One more question, then I'll stop wheedling.
Aren't we going to get in trouble for speeding?"

"Don't you worry, don't give it a thought,"
I do this all the time, and I never get caught,"
Ron Ronda told her with a grin.

Penny and Mark could tell they were going away from the center of the city. They began to notice a change in the areas they were passing through. The belts they rode got narrower. This must be the countryside, Penny thought.

It was almost dark when they reached the end of the last belt. They hadn't seen any houses for a while. Ahead of them in the dusk loomed the outline of a great forest.

Ron Ronda led them toward the trees at a run.

*"We have to get as far from the walkway as we
   can,
Or they'll catch us in the morning, even if we
   ran."*

He panted as they came to the edge of the trees. Then, for the first time, he seemed to lose his confidence. He looked at the dark, dense forest with doubt and fear.

I wonder if he's ever been in a forest like this, Penny thought. We haven't seen a single tree anywhere we've been. Maybe they just don't have them, except for way out here.

"I'll lead the way," she said. She plunged into the darkness between the trees. Mark followed behind her and Ron Ronda came last. Penny held her arms straight out in front of her to keep from bumping into trees she couldn't see. The stones and twigs on the ground hurt her feet. More than once she stubbed her toe on a root. She regretted leaving her shoes back at the house. But she kept on, knowing that they had to go as far into the forest as possible.

After what seemed like hours of groping through

branches and bushes in the darkness, Penny called a halt. All three slumped to the ground exhausted. "I wonder how far we've come," Penny asked after several minutes. Then she noticed that Mark had already fallen asleep. Ron Ronda was soon sleeping too.

Penny tugged off her plastic head mask. It felt good to be free of it. She shook her head a couple of times, swishing her ponytail back and forth, just to remember how it felt to have hair. She checked to make sure the dollar bills were still in place under the elastic band that held her ponytail.

She thought about Dr. Kayla. Will she find out how to send us back? she wondered. What will we do if she doesn't? I don't know if we can stay one step ahead of the lab police like this forever. It'll be pretty tough, living on the run. But definitely better than living under Mac Maxta's thumb!

Then Penny thought of her parents. They seemed a million miles away. It's actually farther than that, Penny reminded herself sadly. She thought of the dinner table. Her mother and father would be sitting there. They would be looking at the empty places for Mark and Penny. She cried a little bit. And then she too curled up and fell asleep.

Penny was dreaming of a giant speeding conveyor belt. It carried her farther and farther into the future. She tried to run backwards on it, back into the past. She tried to run back to her family and her friends. Tree branches slapped her in the face. Though the belt was smooth, she kept stubbing her toes. No matter how hard she ran, the belt still carried her into the future. She couldn't get off. Finally she just collapsed. She lay sobbing as the belt rolled her further and further into the unknown. The wind whistled in her ears.

Penny woke up with a start. There *was* something blowing in her ear! She opened her eyes and looked up. A dog as big as a German shepherd stood over her. He was sniffing at her!

Penny yelled, but the dog didn't look alarmed or excited. He backed off a few paces. Then he calmly turned and walked to the edge of the little clearing. The dog sat there panting slightly and looked back at Penny.

Then Penny noticed the figure standing in the shadows behind the dog. She couldn't see the face, but she could tell that the figure had hair— lots of it. And maybe a beard, too. The man was quite tall. Whatever he was wearing, it wasn't the colored suit that everyone else had.

"Hello," Penny gulped. She reached over to shake Mark and Ron Ronda. They rubbed their eyes and slowly sat up. The tall figure remained in the shadows. And the dog just sat with its tongue hanging out of its mouth.

"Hello," Penny tried again. "Who are you?" Still no answer. Mark and Ron Ronda were wide awake now. She could see that they were both as frightened as she was. "We are, that is, my name in Penny. And, uh, this is Mark. Mark and Ron Ronda. We—we need a place to hide." Whoever the stranger was, he was clearly not the lab police.

The tall figure grunted, and shifted his feet. "Where'd you get that hair?" he asked from the shadows.

Penny's hand flew to her ponytail. "I grew it," she answered.

"Not in the city you didn't," the tall man said.

"No," Penny admitted, "not there. In my own city, where I live. Or used to live."

"And where is that?" the tall man demanded gruffly.

"Five hundred years ago!" Mark burst in. "How come you don't rhyme like everyone else around here?"

"Because I choose not to," was the reply. The man stepped out of the shadows and into the sunlight. Penny gasped. He looked like something out of the past. Not just the past of Ron Ronda and Dr. Kayla, but Penny's and Mark's past too.

The man's thick hair fell to his shoulders. He had a tan face with great craggy eyebrows, a long straight nose, blue eyes, and a full beard. He wore a rough shirt made from animal skins patched together. He had pants of the same material. Soft moccasins covered his feet. He looked like a fur trapper or a frontiersman from the Old West!

"Did you come through the Timeworks too?" Mark asked him happily. Here at least was someone who looked halfway normal.

"No. I have always lived here." The man pointed to the forest around him. "Except for a few years growing up in the city. Bah!" He spat on the ground.

Penny didn't feel so afraid of him anymore. Maybe he would help them find a safe hiding place until they needed to see Dr. Kayla again. Mark had lost his fear, too. He pulled off his head mask with a sigh of relief and shook his hair. Ron Ronda was now the only one in the little clearing with a bald head.

And Ron Ronda was badly frightened, Penny could see. The stranger saw her look at Ron. "It's my dog he's afraid of," he told her. "They don't have them in the city. They don't have any animals at all. Just a lot of shaved-head so-and-so's running around spouting poetry at each other." He spat again.

"It's OK," Penny told Ron Ronda. "He won't hurt you. What's the dog's name?" she asked the stranger.

"Gabe," he replied.

"Come here, Gabe," Penny called. The big dog padded over to her and sniffed her outstretched hand. Then he let her scratch him behind the ears. "Do you want to touch him, Ron Ronda?" The boy shook his head. "Well, maybe later then."

It's funny, Penny thought. This kid was so eager to take on the lab police. He raced around the city on those belts. But last night he was afraid to go into the forest. And now he's frightened of Gabe even though the dog wouldn't hurt him.

"What's your name?" Mark was asking the stranger. "How come you don't live in the city anymore? Where did you get Gabe?"

"I left the city because I was disgusted," the stranger replied. "I found Gabe starving in the woods. People stopped keeping dogs long ago. The forest was the last refuge for a few wild ones. Now there isn't even enough game here to keep them alive. If I didn't catch squirrels and frogs for Gabe, he'd starve too. Maybe that's why he sticks with me."

It took Mark a minute to take in all this information. And talking so much at one stretch seemed to tire the stranger. "You still haven't told us your name," Mark remembered.

"Don't have a name," growled the stranger.

"How come?"

"Nobody here to call me by my name or otherwise. Gabe's only got a name because I talk to him, sometimes. But he doesn't need a name to know who I am, does he?" Gabe blinked and licked his jaws with his long pink tongue.

"But you must have a name, a name that must rhyme,
"To go on without one, that would be a crime!"
protested Ron Ronda.

"I don't need a name and I don't need a rhyme!" the stranger exploded angrily. "And I don't need a lot of high and mighty pointy-head scientists telling me what to do! To shave my head, because only animals have hair! Because human beings don't need it anymore! Hah! A lot of fancy claptrap mucky muck!"

"Claptrap mucky muck?" Mark chuckled. "You aren't such a bad rhymer after all."

The stranger scowled at him and turned to walk back into the forest. Gabe immediately trotted after him. Just as he entered the shadows, the stranger called to them over his shoulder. "If you're still looking for a safe place to stay, I might be able to help you."

Mark needed no encouragement. He bounded off through the trees after man and dog. "C'mon, Ron Ronda," Penny said. "You did a great job getting us away from the drones. But I think we're going to need some more help here. I don't know how to survive in the forest, do you?"

He shook his head. Then he grinned.

"This man is stranger than you or your brother.
If she knew where I was, this would really scare my mother!"

"She's probably scared enough as it is, not knowing where you are," Penny told him. She shuddered. What about my mother? What's she going through? Penny tried to shut away her thoughts. No sense in worrying over something you can't do anything about—yet, she told herself. "C'mon, Ron Ronda. We'll lose them if we don't catch up."

They walked on for an hour through the forest, led by the stranger. Mark had named him Wild Bill. He took them across a small stream. Then he stopped to grab some frogs from the water's edge. They climbed through densely wooded hills. They finally came to the rocky top of a hill which looked out over miles and miles of forest. Wild Bill showed them a cave hidden in the rock.

"This ought to do. The lab police never come here anyway. Sometimes a drone will fly over— there's one now." He pointed off in the distance where a black speck was flying over the thick green treetops.

"You want something to eat?" He reached into a crack in the rock and pulled out a pouch made of animal hide. "Have some acorns to start with." Penny, Mark, and Ron Ronda gnawed on the hard, bitter nuts. Wild Bill quickly kindled a fire and cooked the frogs on a forked stick.

Penny had completely forgotten about food. They hadn't eaten since lunch at home the day before. Or was that five hundred years ago? The acorns weren't very good, but she ate them. When the frog legs came, she didn't think twice

about sinking her teeth into them.

Ron Ronda barely nibbled at his. He wrinkled his nose and spit out parts he didn't like. Penny and Mark devoured theirs on the spot. Mark was hungrily eyeing Ron Ronda's unfinished portion when Penny had an idea.

"Give it to Gabe," she told the bald-headed boy. "Go on, he'll like you for it."

Ron Ronda got up and cautiously approached the dog. He held the frog leg as far in front of him as he could. Gabe gazed at him with his deep, dark eyes. Then Gabe gently took the frog leg from the boy's hand. The dog lay down and held the meat between his paws. He tore at it with long white teeth. Ron Ronda returned to his seat. He seemed to feel a little bit better about this strange four-legged animal.

"Wild crabapples for dessert," Wild Bill announced. He set a crude wooden bowl filled with shriveled little apples before them. They were dried and tasted sweet and crunchy.

"Next, footwear," said the woodsman. He brought out some scraps of animal skin. "Squirrels," he told them with a grin. He began making crude moccasins for their badly scratched feet. "Not as easy getting around without those belts to carry you everywhere, eh?" he asked Ron Ronda.

"No, Wild Bill.
I'm glad you brought us to this hill."

"Rhyme me no rhymes, skinhead!" roared Bill.

"Humpf! Lot of silly words all for nothing." He went back to sewing the moccasins with a bone needle and rough thread.

"It's all right, Ron Ronda. I'm sure you can't change the way you were taught to speak overnight," Penny told the boy. Ron Ronda was blushing furiously. She had to admit that his bald head did look kind of weird. After the first shock back in the city, she had almost gotten used to everyone looking like that. But out here, with Wild Bill and Mark and Gabe, it sure looked strange.

But then we all look strange, she thought, sitting around in these goofy colored suits. They don't blend in at all with the trees, the way Bill's clothes do. We'll have to be careful whenever any of the drones fly over. They could spot us from miles away in these things.

They spent the rest of the day exploring the hilltop around the cave. "This is fun," Penny told Mark excitedly. But Mark looked down at his colored suit and his squirrel skin shoes. "I feel silly. Like I'm running around in the woods in my pajamas and slippers." Then suddenly Mark sat down and began to cry. "Oh Penny, do you think we'll ever get back?" he sobbed, rubbing his eyes with his fists.

"We're sure gonna try, Mark," she said, putting her arm around him. We just have to take one thing at a time."

We've got to do more than just hope Dr. Kayla will come up with something, Penny decided. That's leaving too much to chance. We've got to do something ourselves!

That night, as they sat around a small fire, Penny had an idea. She reached up to her ponytail and slipped the dollar bills out from the elastic band. Dr. Kayla had said not to show the money to anyone. But surely they could trust Wild Bill. So she handed him a dollar.

"Does this mean anything to you?" she asked.

"Not a thing," the woodsman grunted. "That guy in the little circle has hair on him at least. What is this stuff anyways?"

"Money," Penny told him. "But never mind, you wouldn't understand. Here, look at the other side."

Wild Bill scowled at it while picking his teeth with his fingernail. He pointed at the pyramid on the bill. "I've seen that. Not the whole picture, but something like it. There's a carving on a tree. It's a triangle with a line across the top. There's a circle above it, like that eye. I always wondered who did it. Never saw anybody in these woods but me."

"Where is it?" Penny asked excitedly. "Can we go see?"

"Well, it's a pretty good hike. About half a day's walk from here. And I don't know if you will be as safe out there as you will be up here."

"It doesn't matter. I've got to see it!"

"OK," he shrugged. "Tomorrow, then."

That night, Mark and Ron Ronda again fell quickly asleep. Penny closed her eyes and imagined the faces of her mother and father. This made her feel better. I miss you, she told them. And I'm so afraid. But today, for the first time since we got here, I think we've made real progress. Soon we'll be getting back to the past. Back home.

In the morning Wild Bill stuffed some dried food in a skin sack and slung it over his shoulder. With a long staff grasped firmly in his hand, he led the way down the hill. Mark tagged along at his heels. Penny and Ron Ronda brought up the rear. Gabe ranged through the woods far out in front of the group.

Ron Ronda had lost some of his fear of the forest. Now he was interested in everything around him. He still had a little trouble walking on the rocky trail. He wasn't used to anything except smooth surfaces and conveyor belts. Penny helped him over a place where the trail went down the side of a cliff. She thought about the grassless yard surrounding his house.

I guess they never have to mow it, she decided. I wonder if the kids play ball or any other game on it. They sure couldn't play hide and seek. And Mark was right, we didn't see a single bicycle or skateboard or anything.

"Ron Ronda," she asked, "first of all, can I call you Ron? And do you mind if I don't rhyme? Out here it seems kind of silly." She looked around at the leafy green branches and the moss-covered tree trunks.

Ron Ronda came sliding down a steep part of the trail.

"It's fine with me whatever you say,
But don't expect me to change in a day," he said.
He reached out to grab her arm for balance.

"Don't worry about it. Just talk the way it's easiest for you. But I was wondering, do you and your friends ever do anything besides race around the city on those belts?"

"Well, we did build a belt of our own,
But other than that we mostly stay home.
Watching the screen, at least the others do.
I used to get pretty bored, until I met you."

Penny remembered the soft music that Ron's family had been listening to, and Mac Maxta's sudden appearance on the living room wall. "What kind of stuff do they show on the screen?"

"Oh, lots of things, mostly talking and music.
Information and relaxation, that's why we use
*   it."*

"But what is there to relax from," asked Penny, "if you don't do anything else?"

Ron shrugged as he stepped across a bubbling brook. Penny could see that he didn't want to talk about the city anymore. He was too interested in the new sights and sounds all around him. "Look, there's a squirrel," she pointed out. "That's what Wild Bill uses to make clothes."

Late in the afternoon they found what they had been looking for. Wild Bill showed it to Penny. Carved deep in an old tree trunk was the outline of a triangle, with a line cutting across the top corner. There was a circle in the point. It looked

like a rough version of the picture on Penny's dollar bill.

"What do you suppose it means, out here in the middle of the forest?" she asked.

"It must be a trail marker. Nothing else it could be," Bill replied. "Looks like it was carved a long time ago. Maybe a couple of hundred years ago. Now we came in from the east. This path right here runs directly north-south. Back to the south, about a day and a half's walk, is the edge of the forest. My guess is that this sign is for something up ahead, to the north. What it could be, I have no idea. This is the farthest I've ever been from my cave."

Penny thought over the situation as she helped gather wood for a fire. I know it's got to mean something, she told herself. Somewhere on this trail, something is connected with the pyramid. We've got to find out what it is!

Around the fire after dark, Penny talked things over with Wild Bill.

"I don't know what's up the trail either," she said. "But I think it has something to do with the pyramid and the scientists who brought us here. You do understand, don't you, that we have come through time? That we really live hundreds of years ago?"

"I don't pretend to understand it," Bill told her gruffly. "The less I have to do with them scientist folk the better. But I'll take your word for it. Certainly you and your brother didn't grow up here. You've got too much woods sense—and hair—for that."

This surprised Penny, who had never thought of herself as knowing a lot about nature. But she had to admit she knew a lot more than Ron Ronda.

"Wild Bill, I'd like you to lead us further up this trail," Penny asked. "Let's keep going until we find whatever that carving is about." She nodded over her shoulder at the triangle on the tree trunk. "I hope that we'll find something there that will help us get back home."

Bill stared into the fire for a moment. Then he turned to her and nodded.

The next day they pushed on. Around midmorning Gabe discovered something exciting in the trail. He ran back and forth into the woods on either side, sniffing eagerly. When Penny caught up, Bill was already bent on one knee. He was looking at some fresh markings in the ground. Wild Bill was excited too.

"A big animal crossed the trail here. Bigger than anything I've seen before. Maybe more than one of them. I can't read these tracks very well. But I sure am going to find out what made them. You three follow the trail. Gabe and I will catch up later." Bill headed off into the woods. Gabe bounded ahead of him.

The three others continued along the trail. Penny decided to stop for a rest. They drank the cold stream water from a tiny pool just above the path.

For a moment everything was still. They heard

bugs chirping in the grass, and the soft whisper of the brook. Then there was another noise that came floating over the treetops surrounding the meadow. It was a low, steady hum.

"The drones!" Penny cried. "The drones are coming! Get to the trees, quick!" They scrambled to their feet and ran along the trail. It seemed to take forever to get to the edge of the forest. Penny's lungs were bursting. The hum got louder and louder behind them. Finally they tumbled into the shade of the trees, and each rolled behind a tree trunk.

Seconds later two black airships swept into sight above the trees on the opposite side of the meadow. The two drones flew straight across the open space and continued on above the forest ahead.

As their hum vanished in the distance, Penny took a deep breath. "If they had spotted us out there in the open in these colored suits, that would've been the end!"

With Mark leading the way, they trudged on through the forest until the sun began to set through the trees to the west. "I think we should stop here," Mark said as they came to a small clearing by the side of the trail.

They dragged fallen branches to the campsite and piled them together. Mark and Ron Ronda sat side by side breaking the branches into smaller pieces. Penny sat across from them.

She heard a rustle of leaves and the sound of something running through the forest. Mark and

Ron looked up at the trees behind her and both goggled. "What is it?" she cried.

She just had time to turn her head when a rushing animal jumped over her. Its soft flank brushed her cheek, and she could smell its sweat. It landed in the space between her and the boys. Then it leaped over their heads into the woods on the other side of the trail.

"A deer! Did you see that?" Penny jumped up and danced around. Ron was so surprised he couldn't say a thing. Mark dashed into the forest after the deer. But soon he gave up and returned. Then they heard something else running through the trees toward them.

Gabe burst into the clearing and seemed surprised to see them. He was about to take off again when Penny grabbed him by the back of his neck. "Oh no, you don't. Let's wait for Wild Bill." The eager dog was hard to hold back. But with Mark's help she got Gabe to sit down. She scratched his ears while keeping a firm hold on his neck.

Bill finally came huffing into camp just as it turned dark. "Fool dog got away from me. Chased the deer off," he panted. "Spent most of the day running after the two of them. I guess Gabe don't know much about deer hunting."

He sat down and slipped the sack off his shoulder. Wild Bill handed round some nuts he had gathered during the day. "Tomorrow we'll eat better," he promised. "From what I saw today, this part of the forest has a lot more squirrel and rabbit than over where I live. I may consider moving. And a deer too!" Bill was pleased with himself, even though he had lost the larger animal. "Wouldn't have killed it anyway," he told them. "Not until I found out how many more there are around here. *If* there are any more."

The next morning they saw another carved sign on a tree by the trail. It looked just like the first carving.

Bill squinted at it. Then he cocked his head. "Drones coming. Don't worry, they'll never spot us through these trees. But I wonder what they're doing out here?"

The humming came from the north. The ships flew directly over them and headed back to the south. "I wonder if those were the same ones that came over yesterday," Penny said. "They might have gone up ahead someplace. Maybe they stopped overnight and are flying back to the city now."

"Maybe," Bill shrugged. "Why would they want to spend the night in the forest, though? Nobody but me is crazy enough to do that. And you." He grinned at the three of them.

After a stop for lunch, they forded a wide stream and came to another large clearing in the forest. Penny caught her breath. "Look, there it is!" she whispered. Standing alone in the middle of the clearing was a gleaming metal pyramid!

S

"Wow!" exclaimed Mark in a whisper. "Look at that!"

The shining silver pyramid dazzled them all. It sparkled in the sunlight. The pointed tip reached almost as high as the trees surrounding it. The smooth, glassy walls reflected the trees and the blue sky above. The pyramid seemed to be floating by itself in the middle of the clearing.

"I wonder if anybody's inside," said Mark.

"If we see anyone, we'll just tell them we're lost. And then hope for the best," answered Penny. "Look for a door."

They split up. Wild Bill and Mark walked around one side of the pyramid. Penny and Ron went the other way.

"It's smooth all the way around," Penny said when they met again behind it. "Not a door, or even a crack anywhere!"

"Except for that," Bill replied, jerking a thumb over his shoulder. Penny leaned around him. She saw something jutting out from the slanted side of the pyramid.

She walked over to take a look at it. It was flat, about the size of a book. Set into it was a small rectangular tray with a thin slot at the back.

I've seen something like this before, Penny thought. In a store? No, but somewhere near a store. I've got it—the shopping center!

"Mark," she called, "come here. Does this look like one of those things they have in the electronic game room? The bill changer?" She had to give him a boost up the side of the pyramid for him to get a good look at it.

"Sort of, I guess," he shrugged, and jumped down. "But it doesn't have any directions. And no place for the quarters to come out."

"Well, we'll just have to give it a try," Penny replied. "It's the only clue we have." She reached up and slipped her money out of her ponytail. She unrolled one of the bills and flattened it against the side of the pyramid. Carefully Penny placed it in the silver tray. It fit perfectly.

The dollar lay on the tray for a few moments, then was suddenly sucked inside. A humming noise came from the pyramid. After a few seconds, the outline of a door appeared in the smooth metal wall beside the tray. The door slid open. Penny could feel the cool air seeping out from the darkness inside.

"Well," she gulped. "I guess this is where we go in."

She stepped slowly inside the door. The other three, plus Gabe, crowded behind her. They forced her to move farther into the darkness than she would have liked. "Anybody feel a light switch?" she asked.

Her next step brought a click from the floor.

Weak lights flickered on around them. The door slid silently shut behind them. "Uh oh," Mark said. "Now how do we get out?"

Penny picked up her foot and stepped down again in the same place. The lights went off and the door slid open. "That's how," she said, and closed the door again.

The lights were not very strong and much of the inside was still dark. But they could see that they had come in on one side of a huge room. The room seemed to take up all of the pyramid. The walls slanted inward to a point lost in the darkness far above. On the other sides of the room, broad steps rose one behind another until they met the sloping walls about a third of the way up. Hanging from the invisible ceiling was a giant revolving ball covered with thousands of tiny mirrors. These reflected the dim light in a constantly sweeping pattern of dots against the walls.

It's kind of like the Chamber of the Great, Penny thought. But why should it be out here in the middle of the forest? The drones! Maybe some of the scientists flew out here. They might have held a meeting here, or done something, and then returned to the city. But why should they come out here? For secrecy, of course. "Start looking around," she told the rest. "We've gotta figure out what goes on here."

They split up again and searched the room. It was Mark who made the discovery.

"Hey, come here!" he called. "Look at this

stuff!" He pulled out piece after piece of colorful cloth from a drawer hidden in one of the steps. Penny ran over and grabbed one piece, a beautiful dark blue. She held it out at arm's length. The material was much finer than that of the suit she was wearing. She swung it around over her shoulders. It was sort of like the capes the scientists had worn in the Chamber, but larger and longer. The edges were lined with an even deeper blue, while the inside was soft and furry.

Mark handed capes to both Ron and Bill. "Go on, try them," he urged. "*See? Just like me!*" He swirled a red cape around his shoulders. "I feel like a king!" Ron Ronda put his on, but didn't seem too happy about it. Wild Bill just looked at his with scorn.

"Is there anything else in the drawer?" Penny asked. She went through it quickly. "No. How about another drawer?" She began feeling with her fingers along the surface beside it. "Ah!" Her fingers touched a spot which clicked open another drawer. "Look at this! This is even better! It's those hats they were wearing! And blueprints, or plans of some kind."

Penny carefully lifted one of the pyramid hats made of thin silver rods out of the drawer. She placed it on her head. Then she studied the pile of complicated diagrams. One of them was a graph marked in years from 2468 all the way back to the twentieth century. "You know," she told the others excitedly, "this makes me think of some real possibilities!"

Penny went off to sit by herself on one of the steps on the far side of the room. She frowned to herself a couple of times. Then she plucked the hat off her head to look at it. She came to a decision. She got up and marched over to the others. Mark was still spinning about in his cape. Bill and Gabe just stood around, waiting. Ron Ronda stared up at the dark ceiling in wonder.

"Well, I think we've got what we need," Penny said. "Let's take off these capes and Mark, you wrap them up. We're taking them back. I'll take the hats and these plans." She rolled them up.

Wild Bill helped Mark roll the four capes into a bundle. Mark slung them over his shoulder. Penny held the four hats and the plans in her hand and stepped on the switch in the floor. The door opened and they filed out into the sunlight.

As they walked back that afternoon, Penny kept looking thoughtfully at Gabe. The big dog loped along at Wild Bill's heels. Sometimes Gabe dashed off into the forest to check out an exciting scent. He hasn't been trained, Penny decided, but he's plenty smart.

They made their camp at the same place they had left that morning. They sat around eating the roast rabbit that Bill had snared. The woodsman told them, "You know, I'd like to take my time going back through these woods. Looks like there's a lot more good hunting here than back where I live. Are you all in any hurry to get back?"

Penny counted up the days they had been gone. Five. "No," she told him. "We have a few more days left. But if we're going to take it easy on the way back, can I borrow Gabe for a while?"

"I suppose so," Bill squinted into the flames. "I don't need him to set traps. What do you want with him?"

"You'll see," Penny replied. She finished her last rabbit leg and threw the bones to the dog.

The next day they stopped early in the afternoon. Wild Bill took Mark off into the woods to set a few snares for squirrel and rabbit. They left Gabe with Ron and Penny. She began her lessons.

Penny placed one of the silver pyramids on the ground about twenty feet away. Then she returned to Gabe. She pointed in the direction of the pyramid and commanded "Fetch!" Gabe just looked up at her and wagged his tail a bit. This was not going to be so easy, Penny thought. She sat down beside him. Penny stroked his head for a few minutes while she thought.

Then she turned to Ron Ronda. He was sitting beneath a tree, watching a spider weaving its web. "I'm going to need your help," Penny told him. "You're not afraid of Gabe anymore, are you?"

"Nope," said Ron, getting up. "Not a bit." He came over to scratch the dog's ears.

"OK. Here's what I want you to do." She marched the boy and the dog over to where the pyramid lay on the ground. "When I give the signal, you put the pyramid in his mouth. He should be able to hold it by the corner. Give him a shove in my direction. If he drops it or heads off

73

somewhere else, you bring him back here and start over. Got it?"

Ron nodded. Penny returned to her original place. "Fetch," she called. Ron put the pyramid in Gabe's mouth and pushed him toward Penny. Then he ran along behind the dog to make sure he got all the way there. Penny took the pyramid from Gabe and gave him a big hug. "Atta boy, Gabe! Let's do it again!" They did it several times.

"Now let's try it a different way," Penny said. She kept Gabe by her side while Ron took all the pyramids down to the other end. "Fetch," she told Gabe. He galloped down to where Ron had set a pyramid on the ground. The dog brought it back to Penny. "Good boy. Fetch another one now."

After they had gone through this several times, Penny called down to Ron. "Put the next one on your head!"

"On my head?"

"Yeah. If you sit on the ground Gabe will be able to reach it." Ron sat down and placed a silver pyramid on his bald head. Gabe carefully lifted it off by the corner with his teeth. Then he ran with the pyramid down to Penny. "Great going, Gabe!"

Penny was finally satisfied. She and Ron sat together in the shade again. "You know, I'm beginning to think we may make it back yet," she told him.

"I hope so, Penny. Even though I'll be sorry if

you go. I've never had as much fun as this!"

"It's been pretty exciting for me, too. But not all fun! Before we got to your house I was scared stiff! And when you put us on that belt I didn't know what was happening. But we've made it so far."

"Penny, why did you teach Gabe that trick?"

"I don't want to say just yet. But I will tell you something. Somebody besides Gabe has been doing a lot of learning too."

"Oh, yeah? Who?"

"You! You're not even rhyming anymore!"

Ron opened his mouth in surprise, then closed it and blushed. It was true!

* * * * * *

The group moved slowly back to Wild Bill's mountain cave. Penny and Ron took their time walking along the forest trail, talking. Wild Bill, Mark and Gabe ranged through the woods on each side, hunting game. Each evening when they made camp Penny went over her lessons with the big dog.

The night they reached the cave was the ninth night they had spent in the forest. On the next day they would sneak back into the city to meet Dr. Kayla. Penny waited until dinner around the fire was finished before asking her big question.

"Bill, how would you like to go back to the city with us? Just for a visit, I mean, a day or two."

"A day or two in that awful place? Forget it. I don't need it."

"But I do, Bill. That is, Mark and I do. We're going to need your help to get back where we belong. You've been so good to us that I hate to ask you for more. But I have to. We need you. And we're going to need Gabe too."

"Gabe?" The woodsman considered this. "But both of us will look like freaks in the city. They'll spot us and pick us up right away."

"No, they won't," replied Penny. "We'll go back in the evening. Everyone will be at home for the music hours watching their screens. They never saw us riding the belts the last time. And we'll just have to take our chances this time. After we get to Ron's house—well, I've got another plan for then."

"If they catch Gabe and me, we'll never see the woods again," Wild Bill told her.

"And Mark and I will never see our home again either," she reminded him. "If we don't do something drastic we'll never get back there. So we have to take a chance. And we need you and Gabe."

"OK," the woodsman gave in. "I guess I can stand it for a day or two. But if we get cornered, watch out!"

In the morning they started walking to the edge of the forest. They reached it in late afternoon. They all lay down to wait until evening came.

When Ron judged the time was right, they broke from cover. Together they ran to the end of the belt. Ron reached in underneath one of the wheels.

"Right where I left it," he said with satisfaction. He pulled out his strange-looking tool. "All right, everybody get on board and get down." He seemed happy to be able to take charge once again.

Wild Bill eyed the belt with distrust but climbed on, grumbling. Gabe was terrified. He would not get on until Mark and Ron hoisted him onto the belt. Penny quickly climbed up behind him. Bill held Gabe's head and shoulders and Penny held his hind legs. They got the frightened dog to lie down. When the belt speeded up, Gabe tried to jump off. But they held him down and zoomed toward the city.

Having Gabe along made the changes from belt to belt a bit more difficult, but they managed them all. They didn't see anyone. And they hoped that no one had seen them. Just as it got dark, they hopped off at the school grounds.

"Not much farther," Ron told them. "We'll walk. I don't think Gabe could handle the Rumble Run. And you probably wouldn't even fit," he told Wild Bill with a smile.

They followed the orange line, which glowed in the dark, up the valley. "I hope Dr. Kayla has come," said Penny. "And I hope your family didn't get in trouble for helping us."

"I don't think the lab police ever saw us that

day," replied Ron. "And I'm sure no one in my family told them." They walked for the next half hour in silence.

When they arrived at the house they went around to the back. The glass doors were dark. "You wait here," Ron whispered. "I'll go in first."

He crept up to the darkened house and opened one of the doors. Soft music drifted out into the night. Lights began to flicker on. They saw people getting to their feet, muttering *"What's going on? That was such a nice song."* Then they heard Sar Sarah's voice.

"A night full of joy!
The return of my boy!"

Penny saw Dr. Kayla right away and ran to her.

"Hello there, my child.
How was life in the wild?" She gave Penny a big hug.

"It was great, Dr. Kayla. And I found out some things that could help us get back!"

"I have some news too, that I know you'll want to hear,
And perhaps you can explain some things that are not at all clear."

Above the other talk in the room, they heard Sar Sarah laughing and crying. She scolded her son for being gone so long.

"There's dirt on your head. That's not a bit cute!
And—oh, my goodness—what have you done to your suit?"

78

Penny tooked down at herself and at Mark standing nearby. It was true. Ten days in the forest had ground dirt into the knees and seats and elbows and just about every other place on their shiny suits.

"Take it easy, will you Mom?" Ron Ronda complained.

Sar Sarah looked surprised.

"Where did you learn to speak that awful way? What kind of game are you trying to play?"

"Oh, Dr. Kayla," Penny suddenly remembered, "we found a friend in the forest, two friends, and they're going to help us - -"

A scream came from the still open glass door. Evidently someone had already discovered Wild Bill and Gabe. Penny rushed outside where the two stood at the edge of the light.

"These are my friends," she told everybody gathered in the door, gawking at the two hairy strangers. *"They helped us get back here."* She groped for words. *"So they're. . .they're perfectly all right, you need have no fear."*

"Bill," said Penny, turning to him, "won't you come in? These are all good people. There's food and a place to rest."

"No thanks, Penny," the tall figure replied. He patted the sack slung over his shoulder. "We'll do much better out here under the stars. This sure ain't grass," he said, prodding the spongy green surface with his toe. "But it'll do to sleep on, for a night or two."

"OK. We'll find you a hiding place tomorrow."

Penny went back inside. Right after dinner, Dr. Kayla whisked her off for a bath and a change of clothes.

Afterward, Penny sat running her fingers through her hair. Since everyone here is bald, she told herself, they don't have combs or brushes. She had washed her hair with soap because there wasn't any shampoo, either. But Dr. Kayla had helped her. The bald doctor liked to touch Penny's long brown hair. And the doctor had discovered some important information.

Penny patted her clean green suit. I liked the blue one better, she thought. Actually, I was getting kind of attached to it and my fur moccasins. I wonder what it will feel like to wear jeans again. If, if, if.

Mark ran up to her in a fresh red suit. His wet hair was plastered to his forehead. "Penny, Penny! Did you have one of those baths? With the waves and the water massage and the air jets?"

She calmed him down, then told him, "I've got some good news. Where's Ron?" Their friend came running out, his scrubbed head gleaming in the light. "OK," said Penny. "Dr. Kayla's waiting for us."

The two boys followed her into the room where Dr. Kayla sat. She was going over the diagrams that Penny had brought back from the pyramid. She typed something into a small screen and the screen spelled out an answer. Penny shut the door.

"Now," Penny announced with a deep breath, "here's the story. Dr. Kayla has found out a few things about the Timeworks. With the plans we found in the pyramid, she thinks she can send us back to the twentieth century. The problem is Mac Maxta and the others won't let her get near the Timeworks. They say it's their project and no one else can run it. But. . ."

She picked up one of the silver hats. "You remember these. Mac Maxta and a few others were wearing them. They're the badge of some kind of secret society of scientists. They're the ones controlling the Timeworks, and a lot of other things too. We were at their secret meeting place just a few days ago." She paused to let this sink in.

"Dr. Kayla talked with the experimentor who ran out on us. You remember him, Mark? Well, he told the other scientists that as soon as I arrived, I gave him the key to all their secret places. And that key is none other than this!" With a flourish she produced her last dollar.

"A dollar bill? Come on, Penny," Mark protested.

"It's true. Isn't it, Dr. Kayla?" The doctor nodded. "Somehow a few of these pieces of paper have lasted all this time, even though they stopped using money long ago. For some reason, the scientists have used these dollars for their secret society. Probably because of the pyramid on them. It's how we got into that place in the woods, isn't it? Well anyway, the shopkeeper told the rest of the scientists that we have one. Now they think we know their secrets, which in a way we do. And they can't figure out how we know so much."

"So?" asked Mark.

"So we need to scare them and they'll give in! Oh! There's just one thing I'm leaving out." Penny turned to the doctor. "Dr. Kayla, do you think you can make something that will dissolve this metal?" She handed her one of the silver pyramids.

Dr. Kayla examined it closely, then replied:

"I'll have to take it to my lab and run a few tests, We're going there tomorrow anyway, after a good night's rest."

"Right. I hope you can do it." Then Penny turned to Ron and explained his part in the plan. His eyes widened with surprise, then sparkled with excitement. "You think you can do it?" Penny asked. He nodded.

"What about me?" Mark complained. "Don't I get to do anything?"

"Yes. You stay here in the morning and keep Bill and Gabe company. Don't worry, you've got a big part. I'll explain later."

The group broke up and headed for bed. Penny slipped out the back door and walked into the darkness. It didn't seem so long ago that she had been running for her life down this slope. "Bill?" she called softly. "Gabe?"

"Over here." She crept over and found Gabe

curled up at Bill's feet. The woodsman was still awake. He was lying on his back looking up at the sky.

"You all right?" Penny asked him.

"I'll survive," he admitted. "The sooner we get back to the forest the better. But I'll be glad to help you outsmart those pointy-head scientists and get you back where you belong."

"Thank you, Bill." Penny kissed him softly on the forehead and went back indoors.

In the morning, Penny was up early. She unrolled the bundle of capes they had brought from the forest and inspected each one closely. Then she took them to Sar Sarah. Over breakfast, Penny explained to Sar Sarah the changes she wanted made in each cape.

Next Penny slipped outside to take Wild Bill and Gabe some food. She found them hiding under the eaves of the house. Wild Bill thanked her for the food and Gabe licked her hand.

Then Penny went to wake up Mark. She told him, step by step, what he had to do that day. "That's a lot of rhymes to think up," he answered sleepily. "What if something goes wrong?"

"I'm counting on you to see that it doesn't. Just make sure you know your lines."

Finally, Penny strapped on a new plastic head mask that Sar Sarah had made. She was ready to go when Dr. Kayla and Ron appeared. They walked down to Val Valley school together.

At the school they caught the yellow belt into the city. Soon they were moving among crowds of other people. Penny was careful to stand between Ron and Dr. Kayla whenever possible. She didn't want her head mask to give her away.

After a couple of transfers, they got off near a group of long, low buildings without any windows. They reminded Penny of the Timeworks. Dr. Kayla led them on a twisting course through the buildings.

"To get to my lab, we turn like that,
Did you bring along your pyramid hat?"

"Got it right here under my suit," Penny said. It was kind of uncomfortable carrying it around in there. But she couldn't risk letting it be seen.

Dr. Kayla opened a door in one of the buildings and they stepped inside. Penny looked around the huge room. She saw metal tables, glass bottles, and strange-looking machines with dials everywhere. She reached inside the neck of her suit to pull out the silver pyramid. Dr. Kayla took it over to one of the machines and stuck it inside a little glass door. The machine immediately began humming. Numbers appeared on an electronic screen.

"I should be able to make what you want in an
hour or two.
But first I have to make this call to you-know-
who," said Dr. Kayla after reading the screen. She walked over to another counter and picked up a small microphone. She spoke into it:

"Lab police, lab police, orange alert!
Explosion in block 17, several hurt!"

Dr. Kayla opened a door leading to a small storeroom. She scattered a few crystals on the floor. Soon the storeroom was filled with smoke.

Ron and Penny hid behind one of the counters at the back of the lab.

Within minutes the lab police arrived. Dr. Kayla showed them the smoking storeroom. All five policemen dashed in. Dr. Kayla threw a few more crystals after them. Then she shut the door and locked it.

"That will put them to sleep for a few hours at least.
Here, take this and check outside for more lab police." She handed something to Ron.

Ron and Penny poked their heads outside the lab door. A black drone ship sat there parked on the ground with its large side door open. Ron marched right up to it. A black-clad policeman emerged from inside.

"Hey, you kids aren't supposed to be running around here.
This is a lab area. Now get out and stay clear."

Ron held out his hand.

"But look what we found,
Lying on the ground."

The policeman bent over to see what Ron had in his hand. The boy stuck his fist up under the policeman's nose. Ron broke the capsule Dr. Kayla had given him. The policeman sniffed once. Then he keeled over in a dead faint. Ron and Penny each grabbed one of his bare feet and pulled him inside the lab.

Dr. Kayla came back out to the drone ship with

them. She went over the control panel with Ron.

"This one for up and down, this one to steer. It's really quite simple. Does it all seem clear?"

Ron nodded and went on checking the controls. He seemed satisfied. Dr. Kayla went back to her lab. Ron pressed a switch and the ship's door closed. He pressed another and it began to rise in the air. Through the tinted one-way window, they saw the lab buildings falling away below them. With a few jerks and jolts, Ron got the drone ship turned around. They headed back above the city. Ron grinned at Penny. "I could become an ace pilot in no time!"

"I'm sure you could." They zoomed over belts and buildings and thousands of bald heads. Ron took a bearing and changed course. Soon they had passed over Val Valley school and were coming in for a landing in Ron's backyard.

The first thing to greet them there was a very angry barking dog. Gabe stopped growling when he saw Ron and Penny dash out of the drone ship. He looked at them in surprise. Penny gave him a pat on the head as she ran toward the house. "Atta boy, Gabe. You're a great watchdog."

Sar Sarah came out with the capes she had been working on. Penny grabbed the rest of the silver pyramids and rounded up Mark and Wild Bill. Ron took the controls of the drone ship. Mark and Wild Bill got Gabe aboard. Then Penny turned and waved to Sar Sarah.

"Goodbye, thanks for everything, we're on our

way.
*Keep your fingers crossed—maybe we'll meet
again some day."*

Then Ron slid the door closed and the drone
ship rose into the air. Penny tore off her head
mask and told the others. "All right everybody,
this is it! Put on your capes. Did you come up with
a good speech?" she asked Mark. He nodded.
They flew on into the city.

*   *   *   *   *   *

Penny stood before the golden doors of the
Chamber of the Great. Mark, Ron, Wild Bill and
Gabe were all lined up behind her. Everyone
except Gabe wore one of the long capes. Penny
was in royal blue, Mark in flaming red, Wild Bill
in green and Ron in brown. On the back of each
cape Sar Sarah had sewn a large golden eye.

Penny took a deep breath. "Ready?" she
whispered. The others nodded. "Let's go." She
pushed open the golden doors.

Inside, it was as if they had never left. Mac
Maxta stood behind his shimmering silver desk.
He was pounding his gavel for order. The other
scientists were arguing with each other. Everything
came to a halt when the intruders appeared.

Mac Maxta's gavel hung in midair. His mouth
dropped open. His pyramid hat slipped off the
top of his head and came to rest propped on an

ear. He gathered his wits and roared:

"*You're back! This is the Chamber of the Great,*
I remind you!
We've got you now! What is that savage beast
behind you?"

Mark stepped forward. He gave Mac Maxta a stern look. Then Mark cleared this throat and began:

"*Lowly scientists: my sister and I were here once*
before.
You made fun of us then. We couldn't stand
anymore.
But we've come back to prove that you're totally
wrong.
When we've finished we'll go back to where we
belong."

Mark turned and nodded to Penny. She looked at Gabe, then pointed at Mac Maxta and commanded "Fetch!"

Gabe hurtled across the room and up the steps toward the big scientist. Mac Maxta's eyes opened wide, and he got very red in the face. He started to shout and back away. Gabe jumped up on the shining table and snatched the silver pyramid off Mac Maxta's head. He bounded back down to lay it at Penny's feet.

"Good boy, Gabe," she told him. She singled out another of the scientists wearing a pyramid and pointed. "Fetch!"

Gabe repeated his performance. The chamber was now in a panic. Members were screaming

and shouting. They were trying to hide behind their desks. A few tried to leave but Wild Bill rudely shoved them back from the door. The burly woodsman looked pretty scary himself, with his fiery eyes, long curly hair, and big green cape.

Penny kept sending Gabe after the pyramid-hatted members. During the confusion, Dr. Kayla slipped into the chamber. As she brushed past Penny, she handed her a small bottle and the pyramid Penny had given her earlier. Penny hid them both under her cape.

When Gabe had gathered all the hats and dropped them at Penny's feet, he returned to Wild Bill's side. Mark raised his arms for attention.

"Now! The first lesson in travel by time machine:
People from other ages are not always what they
seem.
Though we may look like children, we really are
not.
We are top-level scientists, better than any
you've got.
Long ago we founded a certain secret society
To which my sister now shows you the key."

Penny held up her last remaining dollar with both hands. She turned slowly so that everyone in the chamber could see it. Mac Maxta gasped when he saw it, and so did a few others.

"Yes! When you brought us here you could not
have been more wrong.

*Here is final proof that **our** power is truly
strong."*

Penny took out the little bottle Dr. Kayla had
slipped to her. She popped the cork and poured
the clear liquid contents over all the pyramids at
her feet. The silver rods began to sizzle, then
melt, and finally evaporate. In a few seconds
nothing remained but a small puddle and a few
wisps of smoke. Astonished cries of *"My crown is
gone! I can't go on!"* and *"We are lost! At such a
terrible cost!"* came from around the chamber.
Mac Maxta turned very pale.

But Penny and her friends had not finished. At
a sign from her, they all produced their own silver
pyramids from beneath their capes. They clapped
the pyramids on their heads. The chamber was
struck dumb. Mark continued his speech.

*"If you never believed before, you'd better believe
now.
You've riled us up. We're angry, and how!
You see, some of our secrets we never let slip.
The pyramid's only part—don't forget the tip."*

Mark, Penny, Ron and Bill all turned their
backs to the scientists. Now everyone could see
the large golden eye sewn on each cape. The
scientists gasped. Mac Maxta shrieked *"It is the
eye! The horrible eye!"*

The four turned again to face the chamber.
Mark addressed the scientists:

*"We have shown you how weak the new is
compared with the old.*

94

Are you ready now to do exactly as you are told?"

Mac Maxta looked around wildly for support. But the rest of the scientists all cowered behind their shining tables. Mac Maxta nodded weakly back at Mark.

"All right. Our first condition is that with ceremony and gala,
The Timeworks be turned over to Dr. Kay Kayla!"

Mac Maxta tapped his gavel feebly. "Moved and approved," he croaked.

"Secondly, that because of his valuable knowledge and skill,
Control of the great forest will go to Wild Bill.
Thirdly, our great friend Ron Ronda can keep the drone
That he took this morning for his very own."

Mac Maxta tapped his gavel and answered "Moved and approved" to both terms.

"Finally—and I've waited for this a long time, Mac,
You will let every hair on that bald head of yours grow back!"

"Moved and approved," the dejected scientist muttered. He held his bald head in his hands.

* * * * * *

The group was gathered behind the counter of the Trip Dip ice cream shop. As soon as they had finished their business in the Chamber of the Great, Ron had flown them all to the Timeworks in his new drone ship.

"How closely can you place us back in the twentieth century?" Penny asked Dr. Kayla.

"Within a few minutes of the time you left, I'll bet.

But I can't promise it. The controls are all set."
The doctor smiled at Penny and gave her a big hug.

"We'll soon be in touch with you and your brother.

We have so much to learn from each other."

"You said it. I think a few of our old-fashioned ways would do you some good here. Thanks for everything, Dr. Kayla. You were the first person to help us, and you did it all alone. If you hadn't shown us how to get away from the Chamber, we would never have made it." Dr. Kayla hugged Penny again. Both had to wipe their eyes afterward.

Penny turned to Wild Bill. "Bill, I hope you still enjoy living in the forest. I'm afraid your days are going to be a little bit busier now, being responsible for it all. But somebody's got to make sure that the animals have a place to live. And you're the one!"

"I'll do the best I can, Penny. You take care of yourself and watch out for that wild brother of yours. He'll make a good woodsman one of these days. When you come again, see if you can bring a friend for Gabe. I've given up on finding another dog alive in our time."

"Oh, I will!" Bill leaned over and Penny threw her arms around his muscular neck. She squeezed him tight.

"Now don't you worry, Gabe," she said. Penny took the big dog's head in her hands. "I'm going to look for a dream girlfriend for you." Gabe wagged his tail, pawed the floor, and sneezed.

Penny straightened up and took Ron Ronda's hand in hers. "Well, this is it, kid," she said simply. She kissed him quickly on the cheek. "Don't crash that new ship of yours. I want to go for a long ride when we get back." Penny walked around to the front of the store and stood waiting.

Mark shook hands with everyone and joined her. They waved one last time to their friends behind the counter. Dr. Kayla pressed the button on the wall and the shop was filled again with a swirling pink cloud.

When the cloud had cleared, their friends were gone. Penny and Mark turned to look out the front window of the shop. "We're back!" Mark shouted. "Home at last!" He dashed outside.

Penny followed. She turned and let the door close slowly behind her. Well, no more adventures for a while, she thought. No more stirring up a fuss wherever we go. We're back to being plain old Penny and Mark.

In the blink of an eye, the ice cream shop vanished. Penny was left looking at an empty lot. She turned and walked up Elm Street.

"Gee, Penny," Mark asked, "what are we going to do about these suits?" They were still wearing

97

their shiny pajamas. "They'll want to know what happened to our regular clothes. And how are we going to explain coming back without any ice cream!"

"I don't know what we'll tell them," Penny said, putting her arm around his shoulder. She gave him a big grin. "But we've been in worse scrapes. We'll think of something. And look, we still have our dollar bill that scared all those scientists. Let's save it to remember our trip."

Together they turned the corner and headed home.